Note to parents, carers and teachers

Read it yourself is a series of modern stories, favourite characters and traditional tales written in a simple way for children who are learning to read. The books can be read independently or as part of a guided reading session.

Each book is carefully structured to include many high-frequency words vital for first reading. The sentences on each page are supported closely by pictures to help with understanding, and to offer lively details to talk about.

The books are graded into four levels that progressively introduce wider vocabulary and longer stories as a reader's ability and confidence grows.

Ideas for use

- Ask how your child would like to approach reading at this stage. Would he prefer to hear you read the story first, or would he like to read the story to you and see how he gets on?

- Help him to sound out any words he does not know.

- Developing readers can be concentrating so hard on the words that they sometimes don't fully grasp the meaning of what they're reading. Answering the puzzle questions at the back of the book will help with understanding.

For more information and advice on Read it yourself and book banding, visit **www.ladybird.com/readityourself**

Book
Band
9

Level 3 is ideal for children who are developing reading confidence and stamina, and who are eager to read longer stories with a wider vocabulary.

Special features:

Detailed pictures for added interest and discussion

Wider vocabulary, reinforced through repetition

Once, there was a poor boy called Aladdin.

One day a man said to him, "I am your uncle. I will help you."

He was not really Aladdin's uncle, he was a magician.

6

7

Longer sentences

Simple story structure

"I will make you very rich," the magician said.

He made a fire, and black smoke came up. Then Aladdin saw a stone with a handle on it.

8

9

Educational Consultant: Geraldine Taylor
Book Banding Consultant: Kate Ruttle

A catalogue record for this book is available from the British Library

Published by Ladybird Books Ltd
80 Strand, London, WC2R ORL
A Penguin Company

004

ISBN: 978-0-72328-081-1

Printed in China

Aladdin

Retold by Jillian Powell
Illustrated by Livia Coloji

Once, there was a poor boy called Aladdin.

One day a man said to him, "I am your uncle. I will help you."

He was not really Aladdin's uncle, he was a magician.

"I will make you very rich,"
the magician said.

He made a fire and black smoke
came up. Then Aladdin saw
a stone with a handle on it.

"Pull that handle," said the magician. The stone came up and Aladdin could see a black well.

"If you want to be rich, go down there," the magician said. "You will see a lamp. Bring it back to me. This ring will help you."

Aladdin left the magician and went down to the bottom of the well.

At the bottom of the well was a cave. There, he saw a garden.

Aladdin left the cave and went into the garden. There he saw jewels and a lamp. He took them back to the well.

At the well, the magician said,
"Give me the lamp!"

"Help me out first," said Aladdin.

The magician was so angry that
he put the stone back on the well
and Aladdin could not get out.

Aladdin was in the garden
for three days.

Poor Aladdin was cold. He rubbed his
hands. This rubbed the ring, too.

A genie appeared in a puff of smoke!
"I am the Genie of the Ring,"
he said. "What is your wish?"

"I wish to go home!"
Aladdin said.

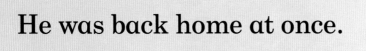

He was back home at once.

Aladdin said, "I must have some dinner, so I will sell this lamp."

"This lamp looks so old," his mother said. She rubbed it to make it look new.

There was a puff of smoke,
and another genie appeared.
"What is your wish?" said the
Genie of the Lamp.

"I wish for some dinner!"
Aladdin said.

At once, they had dinner.

Time went by. Aladdin was now a rich man. Every time he rubbed the lamp, the genie came to him.

One day, Aladdin saw a princess go by and he fell in love with her.

"I want to marry that princess!"
said Aladdin.

"We must go to see the king,"
his mother said.

They gave the king the jewels
Aladdin had taken from the
garden. The king said Aladdin
could marry the princess.

Aladdin rubbed the lamp. "Genie, I wish for a really big house," he said.

Aladdin married the princess and they lived in the big house.

Time went by. One day, the magician came back. He saw Aladdin was rich.

"The magic lamp has made him rich," he said. "I must have it!"

When Aladdin was away, the magician went to see the princess. "I will give you a new lamp if you give me that old one," he said.

"A new lamp for Aladdin!" the princess said. She gave the magician Aladdin's old lamp.

The magician rubbed the lamp. "Genie, make Aladdin's house go away," he said.

The house and the princess disappeared.

The king was very angry. "Aladdin!" he said, "Get the princess back!"

Aladdin rubbed the magic ring on his hand. "Genie of the Ring, take me to the princess," he said.

At once he was with the princess.

"The old lamp is magic!" Aladdin said to the princess, "we must get it back."

So that night they gave
the magician dinner.

"Put this in his dinner,"
Aladdin said to the princess.

The magician ate his dinner and disappeared in a puff of smoke.

Aladdin rubbed the lamp. "Genie, take us home!" he said.

Aladdin and the princess
were back home at once.

They lived happily
ever after with the
magic lamp.

How much do you remember about the story of Aladdin? Answer these questions and find out!

- Who does the magician pretend to be?

- What happens when Aladdin rubs the ring?

- What is magical about Aladdin's lamp?

- Who does Aladdin fall in love with?

- What makes the magician disappear?

Look at the different story sentences and match them to the characters who said them.

"Genie, I wish for a really big house."

"A new lamp for Aladdin!"

"I am your uncle. I will help you."

"We must go to see the king."

Read it yourself with Ladybird

Tick the books you've read!

For more confident readers who can read simple stories with help.

Level 3

- YOU won't like this present as much as I DO! ☐
- The Elves and the Shoemaker ☐
- Hansel and Gretel ☐
- Harry and the Bucketful of Dinosaurs ☐
- Jack and the Beanstalk ☐
- The Red Knight ☐
- Furi on Music Island ☐
- Poppet Stows Away ☐
- Rapunzel ☐
- Aladdin ☐
- The Jungle Book ☐
- Roxy and the Great Escape ☐
- Angry Birds Chuck ☐
- Angry Birds Bomb's Best Birthday ☐

Longer stories for more independent, fluent readers.

Level 4

- I am Inventing an Invention ☐
- Harry and the Dinosaurs United ☐
- Heidi ☐
- Katsuma and the Art Thief ☐
- Luvli and the Glump-a-tron ☐
- The Pied Piper of Hamelin ☐
- Sam and the Robots ☐
- Snow White and the Seven Dwarfs ☐
- The Wizard of Oz ☐
- The Little Mermaid ☐
- Alice in Wonderland ☐
- Oddie The Hero ☐
- Angry Birds Red and the Great Sling-off ☐
- Angry Birds ☐

Available on the App Store

The Read it yourself with Ladybird app is now available

ANDROID APP ON Google play

App also available on Android™ devices